P9-CEN-618

Home for the Holidays

ELISE PRIMAVERA

A Paula Wiseman Book
Simon & Schuster Books for Young Readers
New York   London   Toronto   Sydney

SOPHIE KRINGLE had always dreamed of being the Sugar Plum Fairy in the school play.

At last she'd wear the pink tutu in *The Nutcracker* at Miss Crumpet's School for Young Ladies and Gentlemen. Finally it was Sophie's year!

There was only one hitch.

It was the week after Halloween, which meant it was time to go with her great-aunt Auntie Claus on her annual business trip, and they would not be back until after Christmas.

"Naoh, Sewfay," Miss Crumpet pointed out dryly, "yew cahn't have your cake and eat it tew!"

Sophie had to choose.

That night Sophie was summoned to penthouse 25C of the Bing Cherry Hotel.

"La! The Sugar Plum Fairy! Oh, you'll be *marvelous*, child!" Auntie Claus trilled. "Tutus! Tiaras! I wouldn't miss it for the world!"

"But what about your business trip?" Sophie asked. "You can't have your cake and eat it too, you know."

"Rubbish!" Auntie Claus exclaimed. "What *are* they teaching you at that school, child? You *can* have your cake and eat it too. At *Christmastime* that is the rule!"

Sophie had never heard that rule before.

Auntie Claus stood and took a deep breath. "This year I am staying *home* for the holidays! Christmas in New York—the tree at Rockefeller Center, the Fifty-seventh Street Snowflake, the department store windows dressed to the nines—oh, it will be heaven!"

"But what about your job?" Sophie asked. "Santa would be lost without you there at the North Pole!"

"Red will be the new black, darling," Auntie Claus said mysteriously. "New York will be the new North Pole!"

Later, Sophie had only been asleep a few hours when she awoke with a start to the sound of a great commotion. She snuck down below to see that the elves had come with hundreds of Christmas trees, thousands of ornaments, and tons of tinsel.

There were huge crates of games and dolls, bikes and ice skates, fruitcakes and candy canes and chocolates.

By morning jingle bells were jingling and the Bing Cherry Hotel was more twinkly and cheerful than it had ever been. And it wasn't even Thanksgiving!

Strange guests came too and were lavishly entertained.

"That is Mr. Winter," Auntie Claus said, pointing to an ancient old man. "He's a bit frosty, but he'll warm up."

The old man blew on his hot chocolate, cooling it with a great cloud of snow.

"Does he always do that?" Sophie whispered to her aunt.

"Always," Auntie Claus replied. "And those three all have the same first name, Christmas, Christmas, and Christmas—Past, Present, and Future—isn't it *marvelous*?"

"Can you always see through them?" Sophie asked.

"Always," Auntie Claus said.

A small, thin lady swathed in pink glided by, and Sophie commented, "She looks just like the Sugar Plum Fairy."

"Actually, darling," Auntie Claus replied, "she *is* the Sugar Plum Fairy."

It was the chance of a lifetime and right away Sophie sprang into action. Who better to teach the role of the Sugar Plum Fairy than the *real* Sugar Plum Fairy? But the fairy was terribly important and terribly busy.

"You cannot have ze Christmas in New York wizzont ze *Nutcracker*." The fairy sniffed. "And you cannot have ze *Nutcracker* wizzont *moi*! I do not have time for ze leetle girls."

But Sophie persisted. She visited the fairy every day, hoping to get some pointers, and always brought a special treat.

"Some cake with that latte?" Sophie offered.

"Ze Sugar Plum Fairy does not eat ze cake." The fairy pushed the cake away. "Ze Sugar Plum Fairy has to be as light as ze air to perform at ze Lincoln Center!"

"But Auntie Claus says at Christmastime you can have your cake—and eat it too!"

"*Oui?*" The fairy brightened because, quite frankly, dancing around in the Land of the Sweets every night and not being allowed to have any was really getting to her.

"*Oui!*" Sophie said, and pushed the cake toward her again. "That's the rule."

The weeks passed in a whirl of jetés, pliés, and gingerbread lattes.

By December it was on everyone's lips, from Macy's to Saks, from Bergdorf to Barneys, "Red is the new black! New York is the new North Pole!"

But as Christmas drew closer, New York became colder and colder.

"R-r-r-red is the n-n-new b-b-b-black. N-n-n-new York is the n-n-new North P-p-p-pole!" everyone now said with chattering teeth.

It snowed. It snowed *a lot*.

And then the snowmen came, for it wouldn't be the North Pole without *them*.

In fact, it wouldn't be the North Pole without the North Pole, would it?

The higher the snow got, the more it collected on the Bing Cherry Hotel. The more it collected on the Bing Cherry Hotel, the more the Bing Cherry Hotel looked just exactly like the North Pole.

Sophie peered anxiously out her window. Her one big chance at being the Sugar Plum Fairy was only a week away, and if it kept snowing, the show would be canceled because of the bad weather.

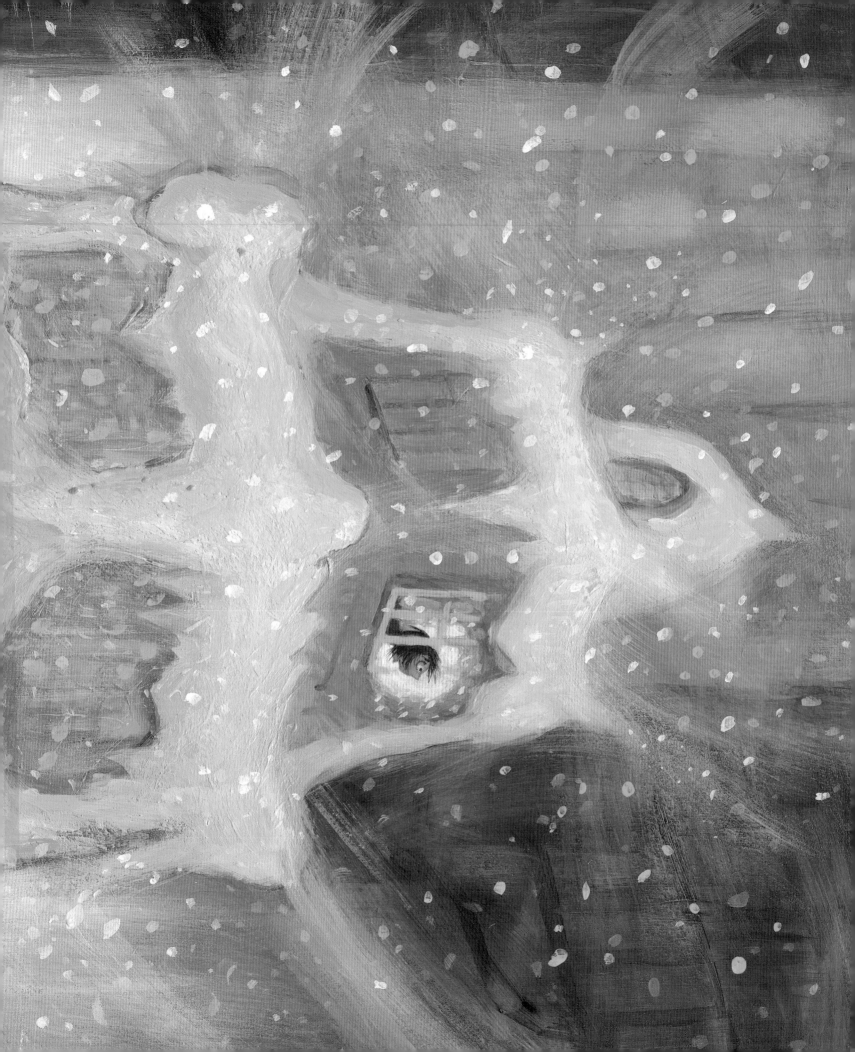

And that's not all.

The three ghosts started showing up like clockwork every midnight to chat.

"Remember last Christmas?" Christmas Past sighed. "Oh! It was such fun!"

"Yes," agreed Christmas Present, "but this Christmas is going to be even better!"

"No-o-o-o-o-o," moaned Christmas Future. "It's going to be ter-r-r-r-rible, aw-w-w-w-w-ful, o-o-o-o-o-o-o-h . . ."

–"Don't listen to him," Christmas Past and Christmas Present said. "He never has *anything* good to say."

But Sophie wondered if maybe Christmas Future was right.

Tomorrow was Christmas Eve! Sophie's debut in *The Nutcracker* at Miss Crumpet's school! But outside another blizzard had begun, evergreen trees were growing tall on 56th Street, and the 57th Street Snowflake looked more like a giant snowball.

So did the Sugar Plum Fairy, who was too fat to fit into her tutu.

"I think you look *divine*, darling," Auntie Claus said tactfully. "Nothing a few slimming vertical lines and a bit of duct tape won't fix."

"New York is NOT ze North Pole!" sobbed the fairy.

"That is right!" grumbled Old Man Winter. "I want to go home! I'm sick and tired of everyone blaming me for the weather!"

"We wouldn't dream of staying, either!" Christmas Past, Present, and Future chimed in.

"You cannot have ze cake and eat it too!" wailed the fairy.

"Nonsense!" Auntie Claus said with a dismissive wave of her hand, and turned to Sophie, who held her own tutu all ready for her own performance at Miss Crumpet's. "Isn't that right, my pet?"

But Sophie wasn't so sure. She knew *her* tutu would fit the Sugar Plum Fairy, but then what would *Sophie* wear? No. There was only one tutu, and it was going to have to be every Sugar Plum Fairy for herself!

Sophie dashed out of the room.

"Remember, darling!" Auntie Claus called after her. "I'll be watching!"

Sophie tried not to think about the fat Sugar Plum Fairy. All the way to Miss Crumpet's School for Young Ladies and Gentleman, Sophie thought about how gorgeous she would look dancing into the Land of the Sweets dressed head to toe in pink. And Auntie Claus would be watching!

Snow was blowing furiously, and it was cold. Imagine an ice cube in an ice cream cone, in a snowman. Now multiply that by a hundred and you will know how cold it was!

Sophie shivered inside her North Pole outfit—the only sensible thing to wear now that New York had become the North Pole. She folded the pink tutu and held it tightly to her.

The wind taunted her every step. It snapped at her coat and snatched at her hat.

The wind plucked the tutu right out of Sophie's hands and blew it away, high, high, high up into the air.

"Come back!" Sophie shouted. The tutu twisted and turned and spiraled around and around the snow-covered Bing Cherry Hotel until it reached the top of the very tip of it.

And that's where it got caught
and stayed, flapping like a pink
flag in the dark, snowy night.

Sophie thought desperately that she would have to climb up and retrieve the tutu! She raced toward the Bing Cherry Hotel, but she was twirled around by the swirling snow and found herself at the back of the building, searching for a way in.

"There it is!" Sophie shouted. She pulled on the handle of an enormous door and rushed inside.

There were elves everywhere and presents—hundreds of thousands of presents! But for once in her life Sophie wasn't thinking about presents.

"I'm supposed to be at Miss Crumpet's in ten minutes. I'm supposed to be the Sugar Plum Fairy, and Auntie Claus is going to be there to see me," Sophie cried. "What am I going to do?"

"You could start by climbing up onto this sleigh," a voice said. "HO! HO! HO!"

There, high above, was Santa, ready for his journey around the world.

Sophie held out her arms and in an instant Santa lifted her with ease onto the sleigh next to him.

"Hurry!" Sophie said. "I have to get to the top of the Bing Cherry Hotel. I have to get my tutu and then go to Miss Crumpet's—I'm going to be the Sugar Plum Fairy and Auntie Claus is going to watch!"

"Then you mustn't be late," Santa said with a wink, and called to his reindeer. "Up, up, and away!"

The sleigh lurched forward and slid out of the hotel. It lifted off the ground and moments later they were flying through the air.

Sophie leaned out of the sleigh. There was the tutu frozen stiff and almost within her grasp. As they sailed by, she picked it from the top of the Bing.

"Excuse me, please?" she said to Santa. "I've changed my mind. I need to make a special delivery of my own."

"HO! HO! HO!" Santa laughed merrily. "Where to?"

"Lincoln Center," Sophie said softly.

Santa guided the reindeer down, down, down, right to the entrance, and Sophie ran to the Sugar Plum Fairy's dressing room.

Sophie looked down, and all she could see was a mountain range of snow-capped concrete.

The department store windows were dark, the Rockefeller Center tree and the 57th Street Snowflake were buried under tons of snow. Great icicles hung gloomily from everything and a frozen mist hovered over the city like an enormous igloo. The northern lights still blazed, for what would the North Pole be without the aurora borealis? But this was not how Christmas in New York was supposed to be.

The fairy was surprised to see Sophie.

"Here," Sophie said. She gently placed the tutu in the Sugar Plum Fairy's hands. Ice and snow glistened on the skirt like diamonds.

But the fairy hesitated.

"It wouldn't be Christmas in New York without you," replied Sophie.

"And we must have ze Christmas in New York!" the Sugar Plum Fairy said. *"Merci beaucoup!"* She thanked Sophie and wiggled into the tutu—it fit her perfectly. "I guess you *can* have ze cake and eat it too at Christmastime—ze rule is true!"

"Au revoir!" Sophie called out and ran back to the sleigh. But she did not believe Auntie Claus's rule any longer. Without her pink tutu, how could Sophie be the Sugar Plum Fairy? It just wouldn't be the same.

"Next stop Miss Crumpet's!" Santa said with a twinkle in his eye.

"Miss Crumpet's," Sophie said sadly.

In moments Sophie was landing at her school. Everyone was there waiting.

"YAY!! The Sugar Plum Fairy is finally here!" they shouted.

Sophie shook her head no. "I gave my tutu away to the real Sugar Plum Fairy—I just can't have my cake and eat it too—not even at Christmastime."

Everyone stood silent and glum.

"Maybe next year," Sophie said sadly.

"Next year?!" Auntie Claus wrapped her cape around her great-niece for a wintry ride north. "Hop on, darlings!"

Suddenly Sophie understood. "Come with us!" she yelled to one and all.

"Where are we going?" they wanted to know.

"On a business trip." Sophie laughed.

As they flew away, the lights from the aurora borealis faded over the angels, which lined the way to the Rockefeller Center tree, which melted and sparkled as bright as ever. The 57th Street Snowflake glittered over 57th Street once more, and the lights from the shop windows shone bright like precious stones. The people came out just to see such a beautiful sight.

From Macy's to Saks, from Bergdorf to Barneys, one and all caroled, "Merry Christmas to you!"

By the light of the aurora borealis, under the real North Pole, Sophie waved the wand with the star attached to it and her tiara twinkled as she leapt into the air in the pink shoes.

"Bravo, darling!" Auntie Claus shouted delightedly. She turned to her great-nephew Christopher. "About next year, my little love," she said. "Have you ever thought about trying out for Tiny Tim? You'd be *marvelous*, child!"

For Nanette Stevenson: dear friend,
New Yorker, and North Pole VIP

Auntie Claus
NEW YORK   NORTH POLE

You are cordially invited to the
Nutcracker Suite,
performed by students from
Miss Crumpet's School for Young Ladies and Gentlemen
Where: North Pole
When: 9:00, Christmas morning
Don't forget to bring your mittens!

SIMON & SCHUSTER BOOKS FOR YOUNG READERS
An imprint of Simon & Schuster Children's Publishing Division
1230 Avenue of the Americas, New York, New York 10020
Copyright © 2009 by Elise Primavera
All rights reserved, including the right of
reproduction in whole or in part in any form.
SIMON & SCHUSTER BOOKS FOR YOUNG READERS
is a trademark of Simon & Schuster, Inc.
For information about special discounts for bulk purchases,
please contact Simon & Schuster Special Sales at
1-866-506-1949 or business@simonandschuster.com.
The Simon & Schuster Speakers Bureau can bring authors to your live event.
For more information or to book an event,
contact the Simon & Schuster Speakers Bureau at 1-866-248-3049
or visit our website at www.simonspeakers.com.
The text for this book is set in Cloister.
The illustrations for this book are rendered in
acrylic paint on Arches watercolor paper.
Manufactured in the United States of America

10 9 8 7 6 5 4 3 2 1
Library of Congress Cataloging-in-Publication Data
Primavera, Elise.
Auntie Claus, home for the holidays / Elise Primavera—1st ed.
p. cm.
"A Paula Wiseman Book."
Summary: When Sophie is cast as the Sugar Plum Fairy in her school's
performance of *The Nutcracker*, her Auntie Claus forgoes her usual fall
business trip and transforms New York City into the North Pole, with
some unpleasant consequences.
ISBN 978-1-4169-5485-9 (hardcover)
[1. Nutcracker (Choreographic work)—Fiction. 2. Ballet
dancing—Fiction. 3. Aunts—Fiction. 4. Christmas—Fiction.
5. Characters in literature—Fiction. 6. New York (N.Y.)—Fiction.]
I. Title.
PZ7.P9354Ay 2009
[E]—dc22
2008051387

* first *
edition